MW01101642

About the Author and Illustrator

Stacey Tucker – writer, early childhood educator, children's meditation teacher, mom and creator of *The Bodhi Tree and Stacey*; a collection of audio meditation stories for children inspired by the natural surroundings and the creatures that dwell in them, near her home on the west coast of Canada. Her website https://kidsmeditation.net/

Tonnja Kopp – artist, illustrator, painter, teacher, early childhood educator, Tonnja incites curiosity and awareness of her love of nature using her gift as an artist. The illustrations were inspired by the forests that surround her home on the west coast of British Columbia, Canada. Her website: https://tonnjavisualart.com/

Walk with Me

Was written for you
with LOVE ♡

Love Stacey ♡

Written by Stacey Tucker
Illustrations by Tonnja Kopp

Walk with Me

Nightingale Books

A CIP catalogue record for this title is
available from the British Library.
ISBN 978-1-83875-436-5

Nightingale Books is an imprint of
Pegasus Elliot MacKenzie Publishers Ltd.
www.pegasuspublishers.com

First Published in 2021

Nightingale Books
Sheraton House Castle Park
Cambridge England

Printed & Bound in Great Britain

Dedication

Gus & Henry, my loves, thank you for choosing me. Love Mom S.T.
Ronja, thank you for the adorable feedback. Love T.K.

Acknowledgements

We wish to acknowledge the promoters of peace & love.

Hello,

Before you begin your walk, please take a minute to breathe a slow, deep inhale, followed by a long, slow exhale. Then another. Walking slowly through the pages of our picture book is an opportunity for both you, as the reader, and to the listeners, to mindfully slow down, get curious and express loving kindness. Our wish is that you experience the calm that comes from sharing your love and kindness with each of the forest creatures, the people that you love and best of all yourself. Come, let's walk.

Squelch, squelch, squelch. Squishy mud under your shoes, only in the spots on the trail where the trees didn't keep the rain off. It's cool in the forest today. The rain has stopped, the sun is out, the leafy forest trees are shading the trail.

To the side you see an auburn fox
scoot by, she looks your way and
keeps going. You send her your
silent wishes. Stay safe and healthy
auburn fox.

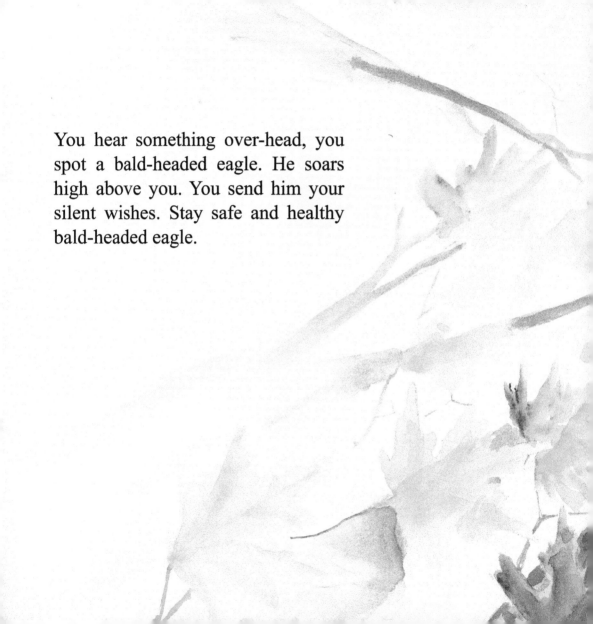

You hear something over-head, you spot a bald-headed eagle. He soars high above you. You send him your silent wishes. Stay safe and healthy bald-headed eagle.

Sitting nearby, nibbling on berries is a stripy tailed raccoon. Her little paws are so busy that she doesn't even see you. You send her your silent wishes. Stay safe and healthy stripy tailed raccoon.

Scampering through the underbrush is a little grey mouse. You only see his shiny black eyes and tiny pink nose for a second, then he's gone. You send him your silent wishes. Stay safe and healthy little grey mouse.

A large brown bear is near. She's looking for salmon up the river so she just stands still for a minute. You send her your silent wishes. Stay safe and healthy brown bear.

As your trail walk comes to an end, take a deep breath in and as you slowly let it out, send all of the woodland creatures your silent wishes to stay safe and healthy.

Take another big breath in and as you slowly let it out. Quietly inside yourself say may I stay safe and healthy and may all the people I love stay safe and healthy too.

Now using our imaginations, let's join the forest creatures and do ten big breaths together.

Breathe in for breath number one. Breathe out breath number one.

Breathe in for breath number two. Breathe out breath number two.

Breathe in for breath number three. Breathe out breath number three.

Breathe in for breath number four. Breathe out breath number four.

Breathe in for breath number five. Breathe out breath number five.

Breathe in for breath number six. Breathe out breath number six.

Breathe in for breath number seven. Breathe out breath number seven.

Breathe in for breath number eight. Breathe out breath number eight.

Breathe in for breath number nine. Breathe out breath number nine.

Breathe in for breath number ten. Breathe out breath number ten.

By calming our bodies with our breath and sharing our loving kindness with the earth's creatures, we make the world a more peaceful place.

Thank you for walking with us, we hope to see you on the trail again soon. Love,

Stacey and Tonnja

CPSIA information can be obtained
at www.ICGtesting.com
Printed in the USA
BVHW020735031221
622835BV00006B/13